Balancing Act

Written by Ali Sparkes
Illustrated by Chris Chalik

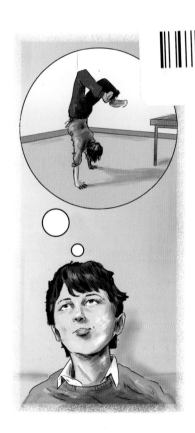

Collins

Newbies

Lara stood at the school gates, giving her mum a discreet little wave.

"Byeeee, sweetheart! Have a fab first day!" yelled Mum from across the road.

She cringed as all the pupils around her turned to stare. Some were rolling their eyes at each other and laughing.

"Sweeeeetheart! Have a fab first day!" mimicked a tall boy with fair hair.

She'd tried to convince Mum not to come with her. "Nobody goes in with their mum past Year Three! I'm not a little kid!" But Mum had insisted because it was her first day. She had at least agreed to stop across the road and not actually come through the school gates.

But her departing shout-out had been very nearly as bad.

Keeping her head down, Lara walked through the playground and straight into reception, as she'd been told to. She had to report there before being taken to her class to be introduced.

She shuddered. She always hated this bit. With Dad in the army, they'd moved house five times in the past ten years. Starting a new school never got any easier.

"You'll love it at Holbrook," Mum had reassured her over toast and marmalade that morning. "It seems very friendly. I know it's a bit scary, but you'll be fine. Why don't you take Calico Kate with you for luck?" She picked up a small rag doll with woollen bunches, button eyes and a blue pinafore dress – something she'd made for Lara many years ago.

"Mum! I'm in Year Six – not Reception!" protested Lara.

"I don't mean you should clutch her to your cheek, suck your thumb and dribble in her hair all day!" said Mum, waving Calico Kate's little cotton-stitched hands. "Just put her in your bag, tucked away, as a secret. It'll make you feel better."

"Honestly, Mum – I'm fine!" said Lara. "I don't need a lucky mascot." But she'd given Calico Kate a little hug before she put her back on her shelf. She just wished Mum would stop making such a big thing of it all. It didn't help.

To Lara's surprise, when she got to reception, she was seated in a small lobby next to another new pupil, a boy with thick dark hair that flopped across his brown eyes. "This is Nicolai Cuvello," explained the receptionist with a cheery smile. "He's going to be in your class too – so you'll be able to look out for each other: two newbies!"

Nicolai and Lara looked at each other awkwardly. They were in Year Six. They were a boy and a girl. And they'd never met before. Did this woman know nothing? thought Lara.

"Hi," mumbled the boy. "It's, um, just Nico, actually."

"Oh. Right," she said. "I'm Lara." She gave him a tight smile. She knew better than to get too friendly. At a new school, you needed to take your time and work out who was who, before you let your guard down. Yes, he was new too, but she knew nothing about him. They waited in tense silence for ten minutes before a tall woman with dark red hair arrived.

"I'm Mrs Toynbee, your teacher," she said, with a bright smile. "I was going to have a bit of a chat with you both, but I'm afraid my assistant's off today and there's no cover, so you'll just have to go in at the deep end. Come on – I'll take you through."

In at the deep end. Great, thought Lara. Because that's what every newbie wants to hear on their first day. Mrs Toynbee might just as well say, "Look – there's the lion pit. They're quite hungry today. Sorry – can I just spray you with meat-scented perfume? Lovely! In you go!"

Make-up Boy and Rag Dolly Girl

Nico tried to look relaxed and cool, even though his insides felt like they were full of pinging rubber bands. The other newbie looked OK. Her hair hung in a shiny blonde ponytail, swinging back and forth as she walked ahead of him with a new school bag over her shoulder, and she seemed totally relaxed about starting a new school. Still … it might help that he wasn't the only one. Oh, who was he kidding? He knew he wasn't going to fit in and he'd already made an enemy. As soon as he'd gone through the school gates, some fair-haired boy had sniggered at his coat. It was just an ordinary coat – blue, with a hood, puffy against the winter cold. Nothing special. But apparently not the right coat.

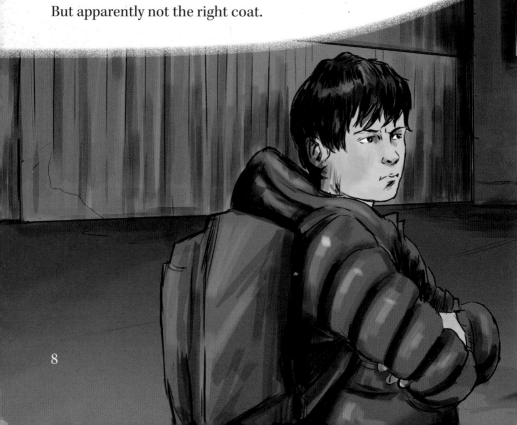

"Look – it's a bouncy castle!" snorted the boy. And several of his mates turned and sniggered too. "Where'd you get that, then?" asked the fair-haired boy. "Down the fair? Oi!" (as Nico tried to shrug and turn away) "Can we have a go on it?"

The others started bundling towards him, grinning.

"Yeah! Let's get on the bouncy castle!" yelled another, and they started shoving and slapping the coat.

Nico turned and stared at the ringleader. "It's just a coat," he said, meeting the boy's narrow grey eyes. "Leave it."

A moment of tense stand-off had been broken by a carolling voice on the far side of the gate. '
'Byeeee, sweetheart! Have a fab first day!" And all the boys turned around to sneer at the girl whose mother had just dropped her in it.

He'd gone straight to reception and by the time Lara had arrived a minute later he was already convincing himself it would be fine. Fine. The fair-haired boy was probably in a different class – different year – maybe. He could be a really tall Year Five.

But now, as they reached the door to Class Six, the first thing he saw through the glass panels was – of course – the same boy. Already smirking at him. In his year and in his class. Great. Just great.

"Everyone," said Mrs Toynbee, as soon as they stepped inside. "I'd like you to welcome Lara Mitchell and Nicolai Cuvello." Around the brightly lit room, 28 faces turned to inspect the newcomers. There were murmurs of curiosity. "Nicolai prefers to be called Nico," went on Mrs Toynbee. "Nico – can you tell us a bit about yourself?"

Nico stared at the teacher in horror. Nobody had prepared him for this.

He put down his bag and stepped forward. And then did a back flip on to his hands and walked up and down with confidence and agility, his hair dangling towards the floor.

"Hi!" he said. "I'm Nico – known to many as Nugget the Clown. I've travelled the world with the Barry Smith Circus and been to about 20 different schools along the way. It's a nightmare trying to fit in, let me tell you! I'm really nervous – especially about the tall fair-haired boy and his mates who mistook me for a bouncy castle earlier. Really freaked out to find him right here in this class. And I can't even hope to move on soon and avoid him, because my parents have lost their minds and decided to buy a house!"

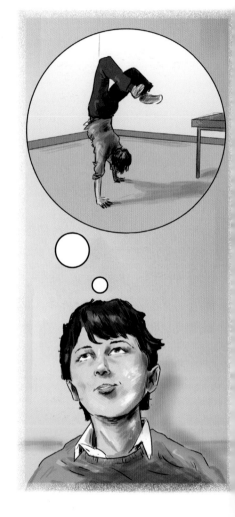

Except, of course, that's not what happened at all. Only in his head. In reality, he stood like a post and mumbled, "Um ... I like gymnastics ... and ... comedy." He nervously wiped his hair off his face and the fair-haired boy put his hand up.

"Yes, Joss," said Mrs Toynbee, impatiently.

"Miss – why has he got white stuff on his head?" said Nico's shiny new enemy, apparently called Joss.

Mrs Toynbee peered across at Nico, surprised. Nico felt a hot surge of horror. No! Surely not. He'd washed it all off last night ... hadn't he? He withdrew his fingers and saw white greasepaint make-up on them.

"Eeeurgh! What's that?" said a girl near the front. "Bird poo?"

The class laughed.

"It's on his neck too!" said Joss. "Did a big bird do a poo on you?"

"That's enough, Joss!" snapped Mrs Toynbee. "I'm sure there's a logical explanation, isn't there, Nico?"

"Um – yeah," he said. Was it better or worse than bird poo? "Well … it's make-up."

The class fell apart.

"I was in a show!" he explained, his voice lost in the babble. "Last night. I thought I'd got it all off, but – "

"He wears make-up!" gurgled Joss, and his mates whooped with laughter.

Nico saw Lara shoot him a look of pure pity before quickly looking away.

"I'm going to wash it off."

He tried to step past her towards the door, but he tripped over a metal bin and fell, grabbing at Lara's bag, hung over her shoulder, to stop himself. She and the bag were jerked sideways. There was a rip as the zip along the top split and her PE kit fell out. And with it fell … a stuffed toy of some kind; a rag doll.

"She's brought a dolly!" squealed Joss, now doubled up with mirth. "Make-up Boy and Rag Dolly Girl! Brilliant!"

Nico sprawled on the floor and next to him Lara was scarlet as she gathered up the rag doll and shoved it back in her bag. "Thanks a lot, Nico," she hissed. "That's it then. We're branded! Make-up Boy and Rag Dolly Girl. Thanks a lot."

A lip stick up

The day didn't get any better. By the time Nico headed for home, his brain was ringing with the giggling and catcalls and hilarious gags that had been hurled at him in the dinner queue and across the playground.

"Hey! Make-up Boy! Your mascara's running!"

"Oi – Make-up Boy! My sister's got some eyeliner you can have if you want it."

And, going into the toilet block: "Off to powder your nose, Make-up Boy?"

Joss and his mates had just about collapsed laughing at that one. It was probably the funniest thing they'd ever thought up. Nico had ignored them, again and again, but they were desperate to get a reaction and just wouldn't let up.

Even in class, there was constant whispering and sniggering and at one point, while Mrs Toynbee wasn't looking, a screwed-up bit of paper landed on his desk.

Wearily he'd unwrapped it and found a ripped-out magazine page – an advert for cosmetics. Scrawled across it was "Fancy some eye shadow, Make-up Boy?"

It was a huge relief to get away from it all and head back along the streets to his new house. The house he'd have to stay in for ever now. He couldn't believe it. He'd lived in a modern caravan since he was a baby, with a different view of the world never far away. The longest he and his parents had ever stayed put before was for six months – two school terms. Some of the schools had been OK. But of course, the one he was finally to stay at had to be this one. Holbrook Junior. And then up to Holbrook Secondary. And in both schools he would forever be known as Make-up Boy, thanks to a bit of white stage make-up accidentally left in his hairline.

He was so lost in his miserable thoughts that he nearly bumped into a girl as she crossed the road and stepped on to the pavement in front of him.

"Oh no," she moaned. "Not you."

It was Rag Dolly Girl.

"Sorry," he muttered, keeping his head down and walking on past her at speed.

But after a few seconds, he heard fast footsteps as she caught up with him. "Look – I didn't mean to sound like that," she said. "It's just been a – "

"Rotten first day?" he asked.

"Well – yeah. For both of us, I guess," said Lara, with a shrug. "That Joss and his stupid mates were giving you a hard time all day, weren't they?"

"Yup. But you too – and that was my fault," Nico admitted. "I'm sorry – about ripping your bag open and all that."

"It was an accident. I blame my mum," said Lara. "I told her I wasn't going to take Calico Kate in to school with me, like a five-year-old. But she just hid her in my bag anyway. Honestly!"

"Parents, eh?" said Nico, with a grin. "Can't live with 'em, not legally allowed to live without 'em." He didn't mention that he had put something lucky in his own bag that day – his fine suede circus performance slippers. Slippers he'd probably never use again. It felt good to have them close, though.

Lara sighed and laughed. "Ah, parents are all right really."

"Yeah," admitted Nico. "Don't tell them that, though."

They walked on in more cheerful silence for a few seconds. Nico was just about to ask her a bit more about why she was also a newbie when there was a chorus of catcalls and four boys leapt out of a side alley at him.

He heard Lara yelling at them as Joss and his mates pinned him up against a wall. He fought back vigorously, shouting, but there were four of them and they held him in place. Joss, grinning and sweaty, pulled something shiny out of his pocket and put it up to Nico's face.

"It's my mum's," said Joss. "But I think it's really your colour."

And he swiped some bright red lipstick across Nico's mouth.

Sad cases

A school trip the very next day didn't help. Lara had hoped to get out of it, but Mum had been very organised and paid for it a week ago. She trailed around the museum alone while everyone else was in pairs or groups of friends. A few of the girls asked if she had her rag dolly with her today and then went off into fits of giggles. This was obviously still hilarious. She didn't think they'd keep it up for ever. Maybe just until next year.

It wasn't the best day she'd had, with no friend to hang out with and nobody making any effort to be nice to her. Then the coach broke down just as they were about to head home. Three minibuses were all the coach company had spare to replace it, so everyone had to be divided up.

Amid the hustle of friends trying to sit together, she, and a handful of other lonely types, mooched around aimlessly.

There were just four Year Sixes and one teacher left over for the last minibus. Mrs Toynbee was in charge of Lara, a boy called Jon who seemed to have had his headphone buds welded into his ears, and a girl called Kim who stared moodily out of the window, chewing her hair. Also Nico – or Make-up Boy as everyone was still calling him. The fun hadn't worn off on that yet, either. Lara wasn't sure which of the two of them was more pitiful.

She didn't sit next to him. He was probably as miserable as she was – he'd been on his own all day too – but sitting together would just make them both an even bigger target. After the lipstick attack yesterday, she knew she should go and sit with him – to show some support. But if she did it could only get worse for both of them. He'd understand that, wouldn't he?

At least it was quiet in here without Joss and his idiotic friends.

Then the minibus door was pulled open again and Lara groaned. Joss climbed in looking sulky. "Got sent over by Mr Frost," he muttered.

"Oh dear. Having a bit too much fun with your friends?" asked Mrs Toynbee, raising an eyebrow. She didn't look too pleased either, Lara thought. She'd probably been looking forward to a nice quiet journey back. Letting Joss in was like inviting a wasp to a summer picnic.

Lara glanced across and saw Nico staring stonily ahead as Joss went past, hissing, "Hello, Make-up Boy!"

Lara shuddered, wishing she could forget yesterday and the lipstick attack. Nico had tried to defend himself but it was four against one. They hadn't hit him. Lara suspected Nico would rather they had. It would've been better than the humiliation of being smeared with lipstick and laughed at. He'd yelled, "Get OFF me! Give it a REST!" Then they'd all stood back and almost wept with mirth at the sight of him trying to rub the stuff off but only smearing it across his chin. Finally Joss had swaggered away, sniggering, "See ya later, Make-up Boy!" and his mates had obediently followed.

Lara had just stood there, looking appalled. When she'd tried to say something he'd turned and walked away from her without a word. She'd felt guilty and stupid. She should have done something. But what?

At least Joss was now on his own and in close proximity to Mrs Toynbee. Even so, the journey home, with Joss just behind them, chewing noisily on bubblegum, would be grim. Nobody spoke as the driver pulled away. Lara peered out of the window opposite.

As Nico stared out of the window at the passing scenery, Lara felt something build up inside her. Anger. Why should she sit here like a sheep? If she wanted to talk to him she should – even if Joss was sitting right behind.

She unclipped her seat belt, got up and moved to the empty seat next to Nico. "I just wanted to ask you something."

He jolted, turning back from gazing at the blurring green and purple landscape. Lara smiled weakly, feeling awkward.

"Go on," he said.

"Why were you wearing make-up?" She glanced uneasily back to the seat behind. Joss, though, was gaping at his mobile phone, engrossed in a game.

He blinked. "I said yesterday. I was in a show."

"What kind of show? Are you in a band? Is that what the make-up is about?"

"No," he said. "I'm a clown."

She leant away from him. "You're winding me up!"

"I'm not. And if you tell anyone else, I'll – "

"Really?" she marvelled. "What – with a red nose and a wig and all that?"

"A bit like that," he admitted. He dug into his pocket and then handed her a small mobile phone with an image open on its screen. In the picture were two clowns; one big, one small, sitting in a comedy clown car, in clown outfits, with bright yellow wigs and thick clown make-up.

"Is that really you?" she said, eventually.

"Yep." He grinned again and tapped the screen. "That's my dad – Beazer the Teazer. And that's me – when I'm being Nugget. It's an old pic though – I was only nine when that was taken."

"You're telling me that you and your dad are in a ... like in a – "

"Not any more," he said, his grin abruptly departing. "Everyone wants to run away to the circus, apparently. But my parents have just run away from it. And I didn't get any choice."

Lara settled more comfortably in the seat, deciding the risk was worth it. "Come on. You've got to tell me the rest!" she said.

"Not much to tell," he replied. "I was born while my parents were working in the circus. They've both won awards, you know – Mum for trapeze and Dad for clowning. I've been travelling with them and performing with my dad since I was four. It was brilliant. I loved it. Up until about three months ago when they suddenly told me they were getting too old to carry on and were setting up an agency for other circus performers instead. No argument. End of old life. Start of new one. Sell caravan, buy house, start new school. Get on with it, Nico." He sighed. "Last night was our farewell show."

"Wow. That must be … really tough," she said, shaking her head. "But … maybe it'll work out OK. Maybe they'll let you run back to the circus when you're 16."

"Yup," he said. "Only five years to wait. Five years of never fitting in."

"I know how you feel," she said. "My dad's in the army so we move house all the time. And we always seem to arrive weeks after term has started. That makes it even worse."

"Hard to know who's winning in the Sad Case race," grinned Nico. "Make-up Boy or Rag Dolly Girl."

"It sounds like another clown act!" Lara giggled.

31

"Clown act?" came a voice right behind them and they turned, with a jolt, to see Joss peering through the gap between their head rests. "Are you a travelling circus freak, Make-up Boy?"

"I was a clown. But I'm not anymore," said Nico, keeping his voice steady.

"Oh what? So, like, you put make-up on and run about like an idiot!" gurgled Joss. "Oh man – I can't wait to spread this!"

"Yes, I ran about like an idiot," agreed Nico, turning around and narrowing his eyes at Joss. "But I got paid to be an idiot and I could stop at any time. You do it for nothing and you couldn't stop it if you tried."

"Ignore him," advised Lara. "Look – wild deer." She pointed outside to a distant brown herd in a clearing between trees. Nico turned to look and nodded.

Joss stood up, checked Mrs Toynbee wasn't looking, took his bubblegum out and splatted it against the window next to Nico's seat, spoiling his view.

Lara got up and glared at him. "What are you going to do?" chortled Joss. "Hit me with your rag dolly?"

"We shouldn't sit together," she muttered, looking away from Nico with a sigh. "It'll just make things worse."

"Oh, right – so I'm too much of a Sad Case for a Sad Case, am I?" he said, as Joss sat back down, sniggering. "Well, whatever." And he turned away and went back to looking out of the window despite the pale pink smear of gum.

Lara felt bad but she couldn't risk staying. "I'm sitting back over there now," she said.

And that was when there was an enormous crash.

And the minibus left the road and spun through the air.

Crash landing

The world turned into a giant kaleidoscope. Lara felt her legs flip past her head. Her arms flailed wildly in the air as a smeary glass window hurtled towards her, intent on smashing her face flat. Only her foot catching on something saved her.

There were cracks, thuds, cries and screams and a bellow of warning from the driver's seat as the contents of the minibus whirled around. Phones, magazines, sweets, Jon's earbuds, their flex twisting through the air like a squid; it seemed to go on for minutes before there was a huge, tooth-rattling CRUNCH and the minibus came to a stop.

Lara lay flat on the window, her face squashed against the glass, but everyone else was hanging awkwardly from the seat belts Mrs Toynbee had insisted they use. Lara realised she could've been a pile of skin and broken bones – but getting her foot caught seemed to have saved her. Although it might have sprained or broken her ankle, going by the sharp needles of pain running up her leg.

"Everyone ... keep calm – " called out Mrs Toynbee, not sounding at all calm herself. "Is anyone hurt?"

There were whimpers as Mrs Toynbee undid her belt and slid down on to the new floor of the minibus. The floor that had been, just a minute ago, a metal and vinyl side panel and a long passenger window. Lara tried to get up and realised her foot was still caught – in someone's grip. She yelped and then Nico said, "Sorry," and let it go.

"Did you catch me?" she croaked, touching her swelling ankle gingerly. He nodded, his face deathly pale. "Th-thanks," she gulped. "You should try out for the cricket team!"

"No problem," he grunted.

"Is anyone hurt?" said Mrs Toynbee, again.

"He is," said Joss, pointing to the driver. The driver lay slumped sideways in his seat belt, unconscious. He wasn't bleeding or obviously injured but his face looked grey and lifeless.

Mrs Toynbee touched the man's neck. "He's breathing," she said. "He's been knocked out, though."

"Where are we?" asked Jon, from the back, sounding dazed.

Lara looked through the glass beneath her and felt her insides lurch. There was nothing there. No ground. Just a sheer drop into a rocky valley.

"Um – everybody," said Mrs Toynbee, with a waver in her voice. "Just stay very still."

See-saw

The minibus suddenly moved, dropping a short distance and coming to rest at a 45 degree angle with a crackly sound and a metallic groan. Everyone screamed. Even Joss. Nico could see from his slightly higher vantage point that the vehicle had shot off the road, over a sheer drop, and plummeted for a few metres before landing on a rocky fell-side opposite. It was now resting, tipped over, on some kind of ledge of rock and plants ... but only up to about two-thirds of its length. The front end, containing himself, Lara, Mrs Toynbee and the driver, seemed to be hanging in thin air. But something else must be supporting it, or the whole thing would be see-sawing back and forth and it wasn't. Well ... it wasn't yet.

"I think you and Lara," he said to Mrs Toynbee, "need to very gently get towards the back. It's safer there."

"What about you?" said Lara, staring up at him, her blue eyes huge and round in her white face.

"I'm … still trying to work that out – " said Nico. He knew that he might easily drop to the overturned side of the vehicle as soon as he undid his seat belt. And that might be all it took to send them plummeting into the valley below. He needed to find a foothold first, then unclip the belt and ease carefully down.

"Just go, very gently," he said again, and Mrs Toynbee and Lara did just that, clambering along the narrow aisle, from armrest to armrest, until they were level with Kim and Jon.

"What about me?" came a voice behind Nico. He turned and saw Joss, suspended just as he was, by the seat belt, hanging on to the seat with arms and legs.

"Just ... stay where you are," said Nico, trying hard to stop his voice shaking. "I'll get down first and then help you down so you don't land too hard. OK?"

"OK," said Joss. Stripped of his usual swagger, he sounded much younger. He looked terrified.

Nico braced his feet against the armrest across the aisle while he undid his seat belt. Supporting himself carefully, he then slid further down until his feet were resting on the metal ledge of the window. There was a long shallow vent which opened up along the top of the main pane. Keeping his eyes off the view lower down (plunging valley, rocks, distant winding silver ribbon of a stream) he flipped the vent open and pressed his face against it, taking in the slightly wider view across the valley. And then he saw it – the reason why they weren't all mush on the valley floor.

They'd come to rest on a cable. A thick dark wire ran across
the valley, from this steep cliff to a rugged fell on the far side.
It was at an angle to where they'd come to rest and somehow it was
supporting the front corner of the tipped-over minibus ... just.
It was probably snagged under the passenger-side front wheel arch.
At least he hoped it was snagged. Thoroughly. If they were merely
resting on it they could slide and ... Nico shuddered and wouldn't
allow himself to think that.

He glanced up at Joss, still suspended above him. "OK – let me
help you down," he said. "Put your feet on the headrests, here."
Joss didn't slap his hand away or call him Make-up Boy as he got
helped down. As he worked his way towards the back, the minibus
groaned and settled slightly further down. There were shrieks
and gasps.

"Help will arrive soon," said Mrs Toynbee, in a rather
high-pitched voice. Nico could see she was very white and shocked.
"Don't worry everyone. The emergency services will soon be here."

Nico looked up through the window above him and saw nothing but the ragged edge of a cliff road about eight or nine metres up. He didn't want to say it out loud, but he wasn't as sure as Mrs Toynbee that the emergency services would soon be there. They'd been travelling a lonely road and the other minibuses, thanks to a few red traffic lights back in the town, had pulled miles ahead of them. At the point they'd crashed, he hadn't seen any other cars. Surely they would've heard other motorists shouting down to them by now, if anyone had been close enough to see? Or seen a few cautious heads peering out over the edge? The verges of the road on the drop side were uneven and rocky. Nobody was looking over them. From the road, it might not be obvious that anyone had crashed over them.

"Can anyone get to their phone?" he asked. "We need to call an ambulance."

"I'm trying," said Mrs Toynbee. "But I think mine's broken."

"Mine's probably in bits too," grunted Joss. "I dropped it while we were looping the loop."

Nico found his own phone in his pocket, but there was no signal. He pressed the Emergency Call button but it didn't seem to be doing anything. Five minutes passed while everyone worked out that their phones were either crunched, missing or useless.

The driver was still unconscious. Worse – he was blocking the only obvious escape route. Someone might be able to get up through the driver's door, clamber along the upward side of the vehicle to the ledge and then climb up to the cliff road. But getting a heavy, unconscious, possibly injured driver out of the way without tipping everything over ... well, it was hopeless. He couldn't move him and he couldn't clamber past him.

There was an emergency door at the back, but right behind it was rock face. There was no space to open the door even three centimetres. Someone was going to have to get out and get help another way. And by "someone" Nico wasn't thinking of one of the others. He knew this was going to be his job. He wouldn't trust anyone else.

"OK. We've got to get help," said Nico, reaching for his backpack, which was wedged under a nearby seat and still zipped up. "And ... I think I might know a way."

"Nico! You can't go anywhere! It's too dangerous!" yelled Mrs Toynbee, huddled at the back with Kim and Jon. Just in front of them, Lara stared as Nico pulled something soft and pale from his bag. Were those ... slippers?

Nico took off his trainers and socks and slid the flesh-coloured slippers on to his bare feet. They were elasticated and fitted tightly, their undersides darker with wear. They looked a bit like ballet pumps, thought Lara, briefly wondering how things would've gone for the new boy yesterday if those had fallen out of his bag.

Nico edged carefully forward and saw a small emergency hammer set into a plastic alcove just below the driver's dashboard, along with a mini fire extinguisher. And peering through the windscreen, he could see the path of the cable, angled out across the valley towards a distant wooden pole set into the fell side. It was just a phone cable. As a circus boy, helping to set up the big top and fairground rides, he'd been trained on safety around overhead cables and wires. He knew that telegraph pole cables were not electrified.

So. That was OK, then. He gulped. And the windscreen could easily be broken by the hammer. He gulped again and closed his eyes … he knew what he had to do. That was bad enough.

Worse was that he couldn't do this alone.

"Nico – what are you doing?" asked Mrs Toynbee.

"Joss," said Nico, turning around to face his tormentor. "I'm going to need your help."

Cliffhanger

"Me?! What do you want me to do?" demanded Joss. His voice was trembling and Lara could tell he was close to tears, just like the rest of them.

"I'm going down the front and smashing the window," said Nico. "Once I'm outside and away along the cable, I'll need you to follow me out and make sure the cable stays in place, under the front of the minibus."

"Nico! Joss! You're not going anywhere!" shouted Mrs Toynbee. "It's far too dangerous. We'll wait here until help comes."

"But what if help doesn't come?" asked Nico. "I don't think anyone knows we've gone over. We've landed at a really weird angle. I don't think we can be seen from the road. And I'm not sure the driver will make it for much longer without a paramedic."

Mrs Toynbee gulped and shook her head so he went on.

"I can get across the cable to the far side of the fell, and then I can climb up and raise the alarm."

"Nico – that's insane!" said Lara. "You'll fall."

He grinned at her as if he'd gone mad. "No I won't." He went forward and grabbed the hammer. "Circus boy – remember?"

"Nico! Joss!" yelled Mrs Toynbee. "Get back here and stay still!" She went to move forward and restrain Joss but the moment she did the bus shuddered and tipped and everyone shrieked.

Lara grabbed her arm and pulled her back while Joss stayed put, halfway along the aisle, frozen with fear.

Mrs Toynbee, on the back seat again, let out a long, shaky breath. "I can't get to you," she said. "So I am ORDERING you, as your teacher. Nico, Joss – do NOT leave this minibus!"

"Sorry, Miss," said Nico, "but I have to."

"You'll be in detention for a MONTH!" Mrs Toynbee yelped.

"Good," he said. "Detention will be fine. Even if I have to share it with Joss."

"I'm not ... I mean, I don't think – " Joss was muttering, glancing from one end of the minibus to the other.

Nico smashed the windscreen.

Lara yelled. "You're a CLOWN! You can't JOKE your way across that cable! If you fall you won't land in a paddling pool of custard!"

"Oh – didn't I mention?" he said. "Clowns don't just drive funny cars and throw pies." He cleared away the shattered glass and pulled himself up on to the edge of the frame, in spite of Mrs Toynbee's shrieks for him to stop. "Some clowns," he went on, grinning back in at Lara, "also do the high wire."

There was a moment of astonished silence in the minibus. And then Joss said, "Listen, Make-up Boy – are you having us on?"

Nico pointed to the suede slippers. "These have seen me across more high wires than you've nicked little kids' dinners, Joss. Now – can you follow me out and hold the cable? It's not electrified. You just need to make sure it doesn't slip down with my weight."

There was a long pause while Joss stared at Nico and then out through the windscreen frame, picturing what he was being asked to do. Eventually he said, "What ... what if it tips up and I fall?"

Nico shook his head. "As long as everyone else stays at the back and keeps still it should hold until I get out on to the cable. It's settled back a bit and it's better balanced now than it was when we first landed."

"How do you KNOW that?" demanded Joss, his eyes wild with fright.

"Trust me – I know a lot about balance," explained Nico. "And cars and vans. I help with maintenance on the circus vehicles. Well ... I did. And I helped to set up fair rides too. I know this stuff."

Nico turned back to Joss and looked at him steadily. "You'll need to anchor your feet. Wrap the seat belt around your ankles."

"This is madness! I forbid either of you to do this!" squeaked Mrs Toynbee but Nico paid her no attention. His eyes were still locked with Joss's.

"Well?" he said. "Are you up for it?"

Joss was breathing fast. For a few seconds Lara thought Nico was on his own. Maybe she could help ... the others all looked too freaked out to move.

Then bully boy Joss took a deep breath and said, "All right. I'll do it." Lara's Amazometer broke.

High wire heroes

There was only a light breeze as Nico stepped out on to the thickly woven wire. There was never a breeze in the Big Top but he'd practised outdoors from time to time over the years, so he knew how it felt.

If he'd been surrounded by an audience with a circus band playing and whoops and gasps of fear below, he would've felt fine. Excited and tense, yes, but fine. He'd done this many times, high above the ground. He couldn't remember the last time he'd fallen.

But the circus high wire was about 15 metres across and about six metres up. This one was at least 40 metres across and too high up to even think about. There was no band, no safety net and no audience, except five terrified people on a dangerously balanced minibus with an unconscious driver. His heart raced so fast he could hear the blood pumping through his ears.

Focus, he told himself, his arms outstretched and steady. You can do this. Those people are DEPENDING on you. The slippers were working, helping him grip the wire with his strong feet. The cable dipped under his weight but not too far. It was stretched tight.

"Have you got it?" he called back to Joss, not daring to look around as the breeze whipped his hair into his eyes and he placed one foot steadily in front of the other.

"YES!" called back Joss, sounding absolutely terrified. He was leaning out of the front of the bus, his feet anchored in the passenger seat belt, his hands firmly gripping the cable to stop it sliding out from the wheel arch and unsettling the minibus.

"You're doing well!" yelled Nico. "Don't worry. I'm not going to walk the whole way. It won't take long. You can let go when I get to the other side. Here goes!"

He ran. Lightly and steadily, his agile toes and expert balance taking him across the valley like a spider on a line of silk. His hair blew back and he felt a rush of exhilaration almost obliterate the fear. Don't look down, he warned himself. And don't get cocky! And then the line bucked under his feet and he heard a cry as the minibus shifted back on the ledge. He couldn't look back. All he could do was manage the wire which had suddenly become a bad-tempered snake in front of him.

Watch it, chase it, out-race it! his mind instructed. You've got across wobblier lines than this before! And it was true. He'd been wire walking since he was four. He could handle this.

He ran fast, outstretched arms tipping up and down to counteract the extra sway beneath his feet, and reached the far side in just 20 seconds. He crashed into the wooden pole and clung to it for a few seconds, gasping with relief, before looking back across his sky-walking route to see the minibus. It looked steady enough and Joss was just letting go of the cable, which had sprung back up under the wheel arch, and was easing back inside.

Nico took another deep breath and then climbed down the pole and on to the steep valley-side. There were plenty of foot and hand holds and in just two minutes he was up on the road. A minute after that, a car pulled over at the sight of the madly waving boy.

"We need help!" yelled Nico. 'Have you got a mobile phone? Please – call an ambulance!"

Wired

"He's done it!" gurgled Joss from his position halfway through the empty frame of the shattered windscreen. "He just ran across that wire! All the way to the other side! He's on the telegraph pole!"

"Get back in, Joss!" yelled Lara. She'd nearly lost her lunch a few seconds back when the minibus had shifted again. Everyone had screamed but the vehicle had actually been settling back on to the ledge and was possibly a little bit more stable now.

"Yes!" Mrs Toynbee urged. "Get in now!"

"I don't know if it's safe!" called back Joss. "I'm scared to let the cable go in case it slips down and unhooks."

"It should be fine now," said Lara. "Nico's weight is off the cable so it's not being pulled down away from the wheel arch. Let it go … very gently."

Joss released his grip on the cable and began to ease back through to the front passenger seat. There was no sudden shift. Everything seemed stable. "Don't slip, don't slip, don't slip," he breathed to himself, unwinding one leg from the seat belt.

Then the driver suspended next to him suddenly lurched, with a loud grunt and a spasm of arms and legs. Joss shrieked and suddenly slid back out through the windscreen. With only one ankle now in the seat belt, a moment later he was tipping over through the frame and sliding down the steep bonnet.

The passengers at the back of the minibus shrieked in horror. Before she could think about it, Lara shot along the seats and grabbed his flailing foot, pulling him back in with all her strength. It wasn't easy, and sharp diamonds of glass dug into her knees as she knelt backwards, hauling Joss in.

Seconds later, they were both sprawled over the awkward tipped-up seats, gasping for air. "Th-th-thought I was a goner," croaked Joss, looking green around the mouth.

"I thought you were a goner too," gasped Lara. She looked up at the dangling driver who was once again silent and senseless. Raising a shaking hand, she checked his throat for a pulse. "He's still breathing," she said. "He should be in the recovery position, really."

"I don't think that's a good idea, Lara," called Mrs Toynbee in a wavering voice. "Please – both of you, come on … slowly … get to the back!"

Carefully, they made their way along until they reached the others. Mrs Toynbee hauled a small first aid kit out of her bag and began to see to the cuts in Lara's knees and some more across Joss's arms.

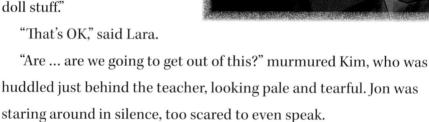

Joss looked over at Lara with an unfamiliar expression on his face. His tough guy mask had peeled away.

"Thanks," he said. "And ... sorry. For all that rag doll stuff."

"That's OK," said Lara.

"Are ... are we going to get out of this?" murmured Kim, who was huddled just behind the teacher, looking pale and tearful. Jon was staring around in silence, too scared to even speak.

"Yes," said Mrs Toynbee, giving her hand a squeeze. "Yes, we are!"

She had to try and reassure them for another 15 minutes, while the minibus creaked and twanged and could have slid off its perch at any moment without warning.

Then there was a metallic thud and everyone shrieked.

"It's OK! It's OK!" Lara peered up through the tipped-over side window and saw a man in a fluorescent jumpsuit, attached to a harness on a wire. He was connecting steel lines and hooks to the minibus and making thumbs up signs at them. Above him hovered a rescue helicopter.

"Don't worry!" he yelled in to them.

"We've made it more secure. We'll get you all out now. Cover yourselves up and turn away – we're going to smash the glass!"

Five minutes later, Lara was dangling in the strong arms of a search and rescue paramedic, clipped securely to his harness. She was taken on a breathtaking ride across the valley. Looking down, she could see woods and rivers and steep green slopes drifting past her feet while her heart galloped around in her ribcage. One by one, they were all plucked from the wrecked minibus, given the extraordinary ride through the cold air and then deposited on a grassy stretch beside the road where several ambulances and a fire and rescue unit were waiting.

Mrs Toynbee was the last one out of the minibus apart from the driver, who needed a more careful rescue. As she sat, wrapped in a foil blanket, Lara went over to her.

"Is Holbrook Junior always this exciting?" she asked.

"Oh yes," said Mrs Toynbee, with a slightly hysterical giggle. "This is nothing. Next week we've got SATs tests!"

Hanging out

Nico walked into the school playground at 10 o'clock, feeling weird. After a day off to recover from their ordeal, he and all the others caught up in the MINIBUS CRASH HELL (that's how the local newspaper put it) were coming back in for a special assembly.

When he'd told Mum and Dad what he'd done they'd hugged him, wordlessly, for some minutes.

Then Dad had said: "Well, we might take the boy out of the circus, but we'll never take the circus out of the boy!" And Mum had nodded at him and he'd gone on: "We want you to run some circus skills workshops with us, Nico. As well as running the agency, me and your mum want to do that, keep our hand in.

We'll travel all over the country – probably Europe too – doing master classes and small performances – but it'll be during the school holidays. How does that sound?" Nico had felt a surge of joy. "It sounds really good!"

Returning to school after all that had happened was messing with his head, though. He wondered how Lara was coping with it all.

The head teacher was allowing reporters from TV, radio and newspapers to come along to the special assembly. It was going to be a media bonanza. All the parents had agreed; they were very proud of how their children had handled the crash. Jon and Kim had been pretty cool, too, and not even whimpered while being rescued by helicopter winch and harness. The driver had been winched out on a stretcher and was now recovering well in hospital. Doctors thought he'd had a heart attack at the wheel.

Nico saw Lara just ahead of him and called to her. "Hey," he said. "Did you bring your lucky rag doll today?"

She grinned. "Did you put on any lucky make-up?"

They laughed. "Some way to start a new school, eh?" said Nico.

"I'd better get used to this one. Mum says we're not moving house again," said Lara. "Dad's leaving the army! He's got a new job in town!" She smiled, not meeting his eyes. "I suppose I'm going to have to make proper friends. That'll be weird."

"Well, I am weird," said Nico. "Put me on your list."

Suddenly four boys stepped out in front of them. Joss and his mates. Nico stopped, suddenly wary again. Had nothing changed?

"Oi!" said Joss. "Make-up Boy – Rag Dolly Girl!"

Nico and Lara looked at each other and sighed. "What, Joss?" said Nico.

Joss glanced around at the others and they nodded. "We were just wondering – " He paused and shook his head as if not quite believing what he was about to say. "Do you wanna ... y'know ... hang out?"

Nico and Lara stared at him in amazement. Lara giggled and put her hand over her mouth.

"Um ... I'm not really a hanging-out type," said Nico, shoving his hands in his pockets.

"All right," said Joss. "But ... if you need us ... either of you. You know where to find us."

"Thanks," said Lara. "Um ... any chance we can lose the nicknames now?"

"Yeah," grinned Joss. "See ya around, Lara. Nico. Come on. We should be in assembly. Did you see the telly people? We're going to be famous – "

Nico rolled his eyes at Lara. "See! He's all nice now!"

"Yeah," laughed Lara. "I only had to save his life!"

"Hmmm," said Nico. "Maybe he'll start helping old ladies across the road and giving sweets to Year Threes."

They watched Joss thwack one of his mates on the head so he could get into the school hall first.

"Or," laughed Lara. "Maybe not ..."

From zero to hero

Lara

"Byeeee sweetheart!"

"She's brought a dolly!"

Nico

"Look – it's a bouncy castle!"

"He wears make-up!"

Joss

"Make-up Boy and Rag Dolly Girl! Brilliant!"

"I think it's really your colour!"

If she wanted to talk to him she should.

Lara shot along the seats and grabbed his flailing foot.

He knew this was going to be his job.

Watch it, chase it, out-race it!

"All right, I'll do it."

"Do you wanna ... hang out?"

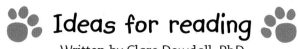

Ideas for reading

Written by Clare Dowdall, PhD
Lecturer and Primary Literacy Consultant

Learning objectives: discuss understanding and explore the meaning of words in context; describe settings, characters and atmosphere and integrate dialogue to convey character and advance the action; use spoken language to develop understanding through speculating, hypothesising, imagining and exploring ideas

Curriculum links: Science

Interest words: carolling voice, agility, kaleidoscope, plummeted, cliffhanger, Amazometer, exhilaration, obliterate, counteract

Resources: whiteboards/paper, ICT for preparing a newspaper report

Getting started

- Read the title of the book and look at the front cover. Ask children to suggest what the idea of a "balancing act" means to them. Prompt them to make a picture in their head.

- Ask children to read the blurb. Discuss what a "newbie" is. Challenge children to predict what the terrifying ordeal may involve, using contextual clues (illustrations, inference from language).

Reading and responding

- Ask children to read chapter 1 (Newbies). When they have finished, ask them to discuss how Lara is feeling about starting school. Build a vocabulary cloud for Lara, to describe her emotional state, e.g. resigned, tentative, anxious.

- Focus on pp6–7. Ask children to find examples of figurative language (tight smile, letting your guard down, in at the deep end, lion pit). Discuss how the author uses this language to create an effect.